© 2013 Disney/Pixar
Published by Hachette Partworks Ltd.
ISBN: 978-1-908648-73-0
Date of Printing: August 2013
Printed in Malaysia by Tien Wah Press

Disney·PIXAR

Ｈ hachette

When Mike Wazowski was six years old, his class took a field trip to Monsters, Inc.

Everyone was really excited about the visit – especially Mike!

"This is where we collect the scream energy to power our whole world," the tour guide said.

Mike was fascinated. He made up his mind to work there as a Scarer when he was older!

Years passed, and when Mike was eighteen, he went off to the famous Monsters University, which had the best Scaring Program in the world.

The head of the program, Dean Hardscrabble, made all the students nervous when she announced that anyone who failed the end-of-term exam would be out of the program.

During his first class, Mike began to answer a question when another student interrupted him with a huge "**ROAR**!" It was James P. Sullivan – "Sulley" for short – the son of the famous Scarer, Bill Sullivan.

Mike thought Sulley was an annoying show-off.

Mike studied hard all term, but Sulley spent most of his time having fun with his fraternity friends at Roar Omega Roar. As a result, Mike did well in all his assignments, but Sulley barely scraped through.

On the day of the final exam, Mike and Sulley argued and accidentally broke a cannister, which contained a record-breaking scream that Dean Hardscrabble had scared out of a child long ago.

She gave them their final exam on the spot, then declared that neither could continue in the Scaring Program!

But Mike had a plan. He decided to sign up for the upcoming Scare Games. The winners would be declared the top Scarers on campus; if Mike was one of them, Hardscrabble would have no choice but to take him back into the Scaring Program.

Hardscrabble agreed – on one condition. If his team lost, Mike would leave Monsters University altogether.

Unfortunately, the only fraternity that wanted
Mike on their team was Oozma Kappa, the school
outcasts. And to make matters even worse, Mike
found out that Sulley had joined the OKs, too!

Mike and Sulley looked at their teammates. It
was going to be a tough job – this bunch didn't
look very scary at all!

The first event was the 'Toxicity Challenge'. The teams had to race through a tunnel filled with stinging glow urchins.

Mike and Sulley left their OK fraternity brothers – Don, Terri and Terry, Squishy and Art – behind and raced each other. The RORs won and the OKs were eliminated.

Then another team was disqualified for cheating – the OKs were back in!

The second event was 'Avoid the Parent'. The teams had to sneak into the library and capture their flag without getting caught.

Sulley almost ruined it for the team by falling off a ladder, but the OKs saved the day by distracting the librarian and escaping.

Squishy even captured the flag! Mike thought there was some hope for the OKs, after all.

Later, the OKs went to a party at the Roar
Omega Roar fraternity house. At first, the RORs
pretended to be friendly. Then they dumped paint,
confetti and soft toys on the OKs and took a
photograph of the result!

The next day, the photo was all over campus. The OKs were so embarrassed! Johnny, the president of ROR, told Mike he and the OKs would never be real Scarers – they were far too cute to be frightening!

The OKs felt like giving up, but Mike sneaked
them into Monsters, Inc. for some inspiration.
"See what all the Scarers have in common?"
asked Mike. "Not really," Squishy answered.
"Exactly!" exclaimed Mike. He meant that Scarers
come in all shapes and sizes.

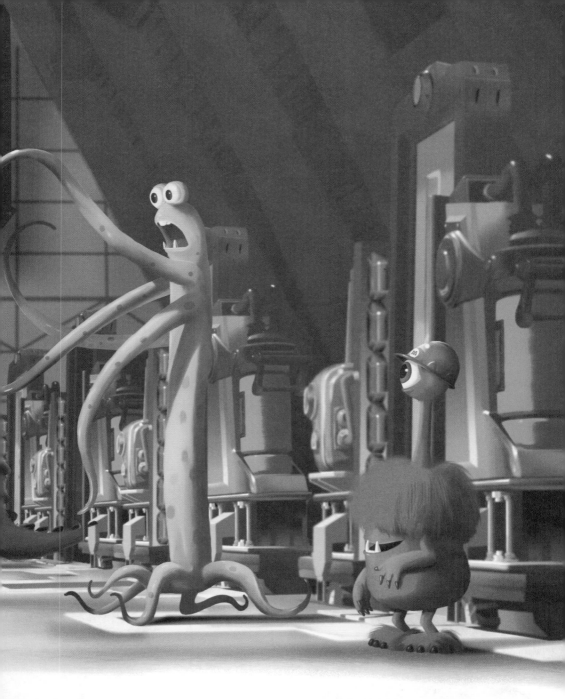

Thanks to Mike, the OKs regained their
confidence. Mike and Sulley realised that from
now on, they had to work as part of a real team,
strong and united!

Mike and Sulley trained the OKs every day. The team did well at 'Don't Scare the Teen', and came in second in 'Hide and Sneak'.

OK had qualified for the final – and they'd be up against ROR!

Sulley worried that Mike wasn't frightening enough to help their team win. He gave Mike some last-minute lessons on how to be scary.

Mike felt more confident about himself, but Sulley still had his doubts.

The final Scare Games event was to enter a simulator and perform a Scare on a robot child.

The teams would go head-to-head and whoever could make the robot child scream the most would be the winner.

The battle was on. Everyone
tried their hardest for OK, but
it wasn't enough and ROR took
a commanding lead. Mike and
Sulley would have to get big
scores to pull things back.

Sulley took on Randy the
chameleon – and won!

Now it was up to Mike to beat Johnny. Mike entered the simulator and gave the most heartfelt roar of his life. The robot child let out an enormous scream.
The OKs won the Scare Games!

Later, Mike discovered that Sulley had rigged the simulator. Sulley didn't think Mike was good enough to score well on his own, so he'd cheated!

Mike felt hurt and betrayed – and so did the other OKs.

Mike decided to prove to everyone that he was scary. He sneaked into the Door Tech Lab, powered up a door to the human world, and walked through.

Alarms blared all across the campus. What Mike was doing was extremely dangerous!

Mike thought he was in a child's bedroom. He crept up to a bed and roared as loud as he could.

The child sat up and smiled at Mike. "You're funny," she said.

Mike suddenly felt many eyes watching him. He wasn't in a child's bedroom at all. He was in a cabin full of campers!

Meanwhile, Sulley guessed what Mike was up to and raced to the lab. When he got there, Hardscrabble was holding back a crowd.

Sulley's friend, Don, created a distraction so that Sulley could go through the door and rescue Mike.

Sulley walked into the empty cabin and heard talking outside. The camp workers were telling some Rangers that the campers had seen an alien. Sulley shot out of the cabin to look for his friend.

"Bear!" cried the Rangers, chasing after him.

Sulley found Mike by a lake.
"They weren't scared of me," said Mike sadly.
Sulley admitted to Mike that he felt like a
failure, too. He wasn't a great Scarer like his
dad, because he was always messing up.

Just then, the Rangers appeared! Mike and Sulley charged towards the door that would take them back to Monster University.

CAMP NATURE

But the door didn't work – Dean Hardscrabble had powered it down to protect the university. Mike and Sulley were trapped!

Mike had an idea. What if they could scare the Rangers and use the energy from their screams to power the door back up?

Mike and Sulley got to work. They clawed and stamped on the floor, slammed the doors, rattled the shutters and overturned the bunk beds.

The door started to light up. Now
Sulley had to deliver the huge Scare that
would get them home again.
"I can't," said Sulley.
"Yes, you can," Mike replied firmly.
Sulley let out a ferocious roar. The
Rangers screamed and screamed…

… and the door powered up! In an instant, Mike and Sulley burst into the Door Tech Lab.

"How did you do this?" Hardscrabble asked in disbelief.

Just then, the authorities appeared and led Mike and Sulley away.

Mike and Sulley were expelled from Monsters University – but the rest of the OKs were allowed into the Scaring Program for their performance in the Scare Games!

Before Mike and Sulley left campus, Mike spotted an ad for workers in the post room at Monsters, Inc.

They got the jobs and quickly moved up in the company.

After a lot of hard work and dedication, Mike and Sulley's dream came true. They became a Scare Team.

On their first day on the job, Mike proudly walked onto the Scare Floor. It had been a long journey, but finally, he was right where he was always meant to be!